The Woman with the Fork

Life inside a psychiatric hospital:

The good, the bad and the funny

based on a true story

Jill Callahan

ISBN 13: 9781733131506

Acknowledgments

For Marcella West,

who was warm and wise,

souled and giving.

and

For Shawn, who gave me

the courage

and the stamina

to write this book.

Table of Contents

Prologue: The Heimlich Maneuver and the Nobel Prize—Letter to Shelly..............1

I Have to Calm Down......................13

Admissions..............................16

Make Yourself at Home 19

The "Quiet Area" 22

The Big Sleep and the Cold Bath..........24

Sometimes You Feel Like a Nut. 26

BB King..................................27

Hal Arthur Prather Meets Frank Zappa 28

Tampax 32

What If He Forgets?......................35

Group Therapy: Theater in the Round..............36

It's Just Noise..........................55

Father Knows Best 57

Almond Joy...............................79

Medications 83

Allergies................................84

It's All in the Cards 85

Elementary, My Dear Watson 87

Wardrobe Dilemma 100

Office Visits..102

Bet Your Bottom Dollar..............................104

ECT...105

CAT Scan..110

The First Treatment: Pleading with my
Sister..112

The Second Treatment: The Jewish Leprechaun
....114

Treatments Three through Eight......................118

The Big Test: Can You Do Your Laundry?......119

Tossing a Buick Across the Parking Lot......122

Jigsaw Puzzle...128

Speaking Up..130

Rude Awakening..133

Missing Person...135

Epilogue: Struck by the Stigma, or
Friendship is a Lost Art................................137

Prologue: The Heimlich Maneuver and the Nobel Prize—Letter to Shelly

September 8, 1991

Dear Shelly,

Hey there, babycakes—I hope this letter finds you well and happy. I'm so sorry I've been out of touch, but I've been caught up in something very strange.

I suppose they told you I'm in here. I know that may seem a little drastic, but I *had* to get away from the things that scare me most—the seven-year itch; the cost of doing business; the lunar eclipse, and the Cat in the Hat.

I've been here for about a month now, but please don't let that scare you—everything is copacetic—I get three hots and a cot and a pile of good drugs every day. Besides, they serve a mean hot pastrami on rye with a kick-ass side of slaw.

* * *

My daily routine is interesting. I go to sleep at 4:00 every morning and wake up about half-an-hour later. I bet you're thinking I must be pretty sleepy by the end of the day, but I can still run a mile like a bat out of hell, and my energy levels are through the roof.

Anyway, sleeplessness is considered a felony around here. The nurses won't even speak to insomniacs after midnight. They turn off all the televisions and lock up the lounge. They think if people get bored enough, they'll go back to bed and fall asleep, but I'm here to tell you it ain't necessarily so.

* * *

As for the living accommodations, I found a special place just perfect for me—it's just a little alcove behind the back stairs, but it's surrounded by papier-mâché tulips and elephant ears.
It wasn't much to look at when I found it, but a friend brought in my

hub cap collection, and it really feels like *my* place now—a place where I can write my memoirs, practice my tuba, and pace the floor.

* * *

My husband brings me wonderful books all the time, which is a real blessing, since visitors often ask how I got here and, thanks to him, I've always got a good story in the palm of my hand.

As a matter of fact, I just finished reading *Crime and Punishment* by Dostoevsky. Man, *that* guy was a strange critter, but he sure had a way with (long Russian) words.

* * *

Anyway, I've had a lot of time to think things over since I got here—things like counterfeit bills; two peas in a pod; male pattern baldness, and one size fits all.

* * *

The dilemma about my brassieres has become the most pressing issue for me now.

Remember when I lost all that weight last summer? Well, I didn't mention it at the time, but as I took off the pounds, my bras became too big. That left me in an awkward predicament and, since I've lost more weight in here, it's still with me now.

The bra I'm wearing today is a case in point. Oh, sure—you might say it fits just fine, and you'd be right—so long as I don't make any sudden moves, but one tiny hiccup and the bra pops up over my breasts and catches itself around my chin.

I wore the same bra on a disastrous date just before I came in here. I went to a fancy restaurant with a high-powered professional man by the name of David R. McCain.

Anyway, I ordered the fish, which was a big mistake because I choked on a bone and David had to use the Heimlich Maneuver to clear my pipes.

He gave me a big slap on the back right there at the table, as he yelled,

"Come on, baby, spit it out!"

That made for some snooty comments from a couple of customers across the room but, after all, we *were* in Princeton, and it comes with the territory.

* * *

Anyway, I reached up to brush the hair out of my eyes and—sure enough—that bra flew out from the front of my dress and lodged itself around my throat.

I was too mortified to speak, but David looked at my bra with a sly grin.

"Here," he said, "let me help you with that."

"Thanks just the same," I said, "but I'm keeping my underwear to myself tonight."

* * *

5

David offered to help me with my bra again when we got back to my place.

"Not tonight, David," I said in a firm voice.

He went silent for a few minutes, but then said he had important work to do at home.

"I've *got* to finish my taxes tonight," he moaned.

"My portfolio is really complicated," he said, "so I have to find a few more write-offs before I file."

He excused himself and went on home.

* * *

God must know why I thought that man would be interesting. I wanted to talk to him about life, love, truth and beauty. He wanted to talk to me about taxes.

* * *

I put on my purple moo moo and big puppy slippers the minute he left. I turned on an old episode of the *Odd Couple* and got out a big bag of double-fudge cookies and a carton of milk.

* * *

The bra I wore that night gave me a big lift, but who wants to die of strangulation by a pair of double-C cups?

That's when my quest for a new bra began. I hadn't bought one for a long time, and I was confused by the engineering and appalled by the prices.

I'd be damned if I was going to pay over $60 for a piece of support gear that would probably back up and choke me to death. Of course, I could always sew a bra to the inside of my dress— just to hold things down, but I knew all too well how things can suddenly backfire and become unhinged.

* * *

Seriously, I had bad bra karma all over me. I told my shrink about it, but he just upped my meds.

* * *

I put my bra aside and tried to stop thinking. I closed my eyes and took a deep breath, but my mind just shifted from rhythm and blues to fine cosmetics. That's where it stalled, so I went to bed.

Speaking of fine cosmetics, my roommate told me Avon was running a sale on bikini wax last month. I'd never tried the stuff before, so I had a few questions. Does it burn to the touch? Does it stain the skin? Does it have exotic ingredients, like magical mud or miracle mulch?

I decided to ask Nurse Hayes about it, since she seems to know a little something about everything. Besides, I don't trust my Avon lady anymore— she went to work at Harry's Park and Pawn a few weeks ago and she's been sort of sleazy ever since then.

* * *

Anyway, I leaned back in my chair, closed my eyes, and thought about Watson—my big, beautiful wonder-dog. That made me feel at peace, and I finally fell asleep.

* * *

I woke up about fifteen minutes later with a question on my mind—a question that'd been haunting me for days.

Why do people name their dogs according to the way they look? "Boots," "Brownie," and "Spot" are especially offensive, since they're totally uninspired and painfully boring.

I have a friend who named her dog "Several Spots."

You had to admire a woman who could think like that.

* * *

Anyway, I'm watching the evening news as I write, and they just announced the Nobel Prize winners for this year.

I'm disappointed.

Why do they always give that prize to physicists, economists, mathematicians and the like?

Why don't they have a Nobel Prize for people in other crucial professions—like beauticians, secretaries, and tattoo artists? They're often the only funny people at the Christmas party, and they try to make everybody else look good. They also work their asses off for little or no recognition and about 50 cents an hour.

It makes me want to go down to the lobby and burn my pantyhose.

* * *

Say, want to go to Paris for after-dinner drinks when I get out of here? We could fly out on Friday morning and come back Sunday night. That should give us plenty of time for a midnight rendezvous with a couple of enticing Parisian strangers.

I sure hope they're good dancers because, if the music's right, I'll just *have* to jump up and shake a leg. Afterall, who wants to sit on the sidelines in the middle of Paris?

* * *

Anyway, I hope you're enjoying the finer things in life, a bra that fits like a satin glove; a good night's sleep with enchanting dreams; a great big dog with a clever name, and a graceful alternative to the Heimlich Maneuver.

* * *

You're so much smarter than me, my sweet friend, so if you have any clues to the quandaries above, please be sure to let me know.

In the meantime, beware of men with "complicated portfolios," never order the fish, and don't forget to accessorize.

Most of all, please look both ways before you cross the street—you've always been a treasure to me.

Love,

Miss Whitney

I Have to Calm Down

They found me in the parking lot at work one day. I was sitting in my car, rocking back and forth, talking to myself.

"I have to calm down. I have to calm down."

I said it again, "I have to calm down."

They called my husband and told him something was wrong. He got to the parking lot half-an-hour later.

The minute he saw the look in my eyes, he took a step back and puked all over the car. He quickly wiped his mouth on his shirt and took a deep breath.

"You'll be ok," he whispered hoarsely, but I was still rocking back and forth, talking to myself.

"I have to calm down. I have to calm down."

* * *

A man pulled into the parking space next to ours.

He'd seen my husband puke.

"You folks ok?" he said, as he got out of his car.

"Yes—we're fine," my husband groaned.

"Come on," he whispered, "let's get the hell out of here."

* * *

"Don't worry," he said, as he started the engine.

"There's a special hospital in north Jersey—it's supposed to be the best place for things like this."

"Hospital?" I said.

"Do we need a hospital?

Am I bleeding?"

"No," he said, "you're alright, but let's just take a ride up there and see what they say."

* * *

I rocked back and forth and said it over and over for the entire two-hours we were on the road.

"I have to calm down. I have to calm down."

We finally pulled up to the hospital entrance, but we sat in the car for a few minutes—trying to find the courage to go in.

Admissions

The admitting nurse said her name was Martha. She seemed sympathetic, so I told her about everything—speed limits; safety pins; football helmets; sunscreens; tourniquets; fire alarms; air bags, and overdue fines.

"Tell me about those things," Martha said.

"I *can't*," I moaned, "but if you see them coming, run like a bat out of hell."

* * *

'Well, at least I warned her,' I thought, as I slumped down in my chair and started to cry. I didn't stop until my husband came over and put his arm around me.

* * *

I took a good look around the room and sniffed.

"I don't like this place," I said.

"It stinks."

I brushed the hair from my eyes.

* * *

"Do I really need to be here?" I asked Martha.

"Well, yes," she said. "It's for the best, at least for the time being."

* * *

"Ok, that's enough," I said, as I got up from my chair.

I'm going home."

* * *

"Hold on," Martha said, as she pushed a form across the desk.

"Sign here," she said, pointing to the bottom line.

My husband took the form and read it over.

"It's ok," he said, "go ahead and sign."

"Alright—if you say so—but it'd better not be a bill, because I'm not paying."

"It's not a bill."

"Ok—then what is it?

Oh, *I* know," I said.

"It must be a winning lottery ticket.

Hey—that means we can go to Tahiti and lie out in the sun.

I bet I could *really* calm down—if I could only get to the ocean."

Make Yourself at Home

My husband walked me to my room. I sat down on the edge of the bed and pulled him closer.

"Don't worry," I whispered.

"*I'm* just fine—*you're* the one who's crazy."

* * *

"Listen," he said, "I've got to go home to feed the dog, but I won't be long."

"*Go ahead,*" I snarled, "*go home,* but you'll never find the phonebook."

"The phonebook?" he asked, "why would I want that?"

"I don't know, but I locked it up in a special place, and you'll never find the key."

"The key? The key to what?"

"The safety deposit box, of course."

"Oh, will I need it?"

19

"You never know—all our important papers are in there."

"And, listen," I said, "if you do find the phonebook, don't go calling anybody about all this—it's strictly between you and me.

Got it?"

"Ok," he sighed. "Anything else?"

"No—I've got nothing else to say— you'll have to do all the talking from now on."

* * *

"Ok, but I've still got to feed the dog. I won't be long," he said as he left.

* * *

Two aides came into the room and looked me up and down.
"And *you* can fuck off, too," I spat, as I darted for the door.
I gave them a run for their money, but it didn't take them long to catch up to me.

They got me down on the floor, but I spat on one and pulled a clump of hair out of the other.

They strapped me into a wheelchair, but I thrashed around until it flipped over on its side.

They sat it upright and wheeled me away.

The "Quiet Area"

'They're going to *kill* me now,' I thought, as they took me into a tiny room, gave me an injection, and parked me in a corner.

The room was completely bare, except for a thin mattress on the floor.

It was cold.

* * *

"Where the hell am I?" I asked an aide.

"You're in the "Quiet Area," he said.

"The *what?*"

"The 'Quiet Area,'—it's a place where you can relax and calm down."

* * *

"I *am* calm," I insisted, as the aides walked out, locking the door behind them as they went.

'Oh, my God," I said to myself, as I drifted into sleep.

'Now you've failed at *everything*.'

The Big Sleep and the Cold Bath

I slept for six days straight. No one was allowed in to see me—not even my husband.

* * *

When I finally woke, they took me into a bathroom with a gigantic tub.

A woman came in carrying a stack of towels on her arm.

"I'm Zelma," she said.

"I'm going to give you a bath, and I don't want to hear any shit about it."

"Yes, mam," I said, as I got naked and slipped into the tub.

"Man, that's cold," I said, shivering all over.

"I know," Zelma said, as she sat down on the edge of the tub.

"It's supposed to be that way."

* * *

"Ok," I said, "but I'm very modest in my *real* life."

"So am I."

"That may be, Zelma, but you're not the one with your ass sitting in this tub."

* * *

When the bath was over, they gave me another injection and wheeled me back to the ward.

Sometimes You Feel Like a Nut. . .

The first thing I saw was the nurse's lounge, so I marched right in.

I could have sworn they'd invited me to join them, but the head nurse pointed me back to the ward and told me to go.

I heard them singing and laughing as I left.

Sometimes you feel like a nut. Sometimes you don't.

BB King

My doctor introduced himself as Bruce Brandon-Knowles, but I knew he was really BB King.

'Some people just have to travel incognito,' I thought, as I tapped out a melody on the table. I tossed my head back and crooned my favorite BB King song:

Nobody loves me but my mama, and she could be jiving too.

"That's a catchy tune," BB said.

"Where did you hear that?"

"It's a secret," I said, "and I'm not telling."

Hal Arthur Prather Meets Frank Zappa

A little bald man introduced himself by his full name and title.

"Hi there," he said, reaching out to shake my hand.

"Hal Arthur Prather here, Director of Social and Recreational Programs."

I couldn't figure out why, but Hal looked sort of strange.

'Maybe he's got some sort of physical ailment,' I thought.

'Or maybe it's all that greasy kid's stuff on his bare scalp. (I swear, you could have fried a couple of eggs up there.)

'No, that's not it,' I thought.

'*I know*—he must be a former patient—he certainly looks edgy enough.'

* * *

Anyway, I watched Hal closely for a couple of days.

Mostly he just roamed around the halls and talked to people a lot.

One night he made an announcement over the PA system.

"Hey kids," he said.

"Hal Arthur Prather here.

Listen, basket weaving class starts in fifteen minutes, and I *know* you don't want to miss *that* one"

Hal chuckled to himself. He did that a lot. I couldn't figure out what was so funny, but I guess if you're the Director of Social and Recreational Programs, you *have* to laugh a lot.

* * *

Anyway, Hal played Muzak over the PA system early every morning, which was completely offensive, if you ask me.

He put on some watered-down jazz one morning and made an announcement:

"Hey, boys and girls—Hal Arthur Prather here.

Let's go to breakfast with a cruise you can't lose—and don't forget to give a great big smile to everyone you meet."

* * *

Hal irritated the shit out of me. Every time I heard his voice come over the PA system, I wanted to do him harm.

'Wait a minute,' I thought, after one of his particularly obnoxious announcements—I'm a paying customer here—I don't have to put up with this shit.'

I went to the phone, called my husband, and asked him to bring in a special CD from home.

He brought it with him that night, and I tucked it carefully inside my purse.

* * *

The next morning the door to Hal's office was wide open, but there was no one around.

I crept in quietly, put the CD in the player, and hit 'start.'

I hurried down the hall to the women's yoga class. They'd just assumed the lotus position when Frank Zappa suddenly belted out a tune:

Watch out where the huskies go, and don't you eat that yellow snow.

About a dozen women moved toward the speakers in the front of the room.

Most of them looked bewildered, but three or four were doubled over—laughing and crying at the same time.

One woman swore out loud,
"Oh, *shit,*" she said,
"*Don't* make me laugh—my *Depends* are
already begging for mercy."

* * *

Hal Arthur Prather almost ruptured
a hemorrhoid as he ran down the hall.
"Stop that!" he screamed.
"Stop that music!"

Tampax

I woke up one morning with terrible cramps—cramps so bad they made me want to file my nails with a hack saw and dye my hair green.

I staggered down the hall, looking for Wendy—the friendliest nurse on the ward.

"I need tampax," I groaned.

Wendy nodded and gave me a wink.

"I understand," she said.

"I've got mine too."

It was as if we were sharing a special secret—just between friends.

* * *

Anyway, there were about a dozen patients in the lounge that night. I was still new to the ward, so they wanted to check me out.

They gathered around and started asking questions.

"Where do you live?

Are you married?

Why are you here?"

The nurses had warned me not to give out personal information to other patients, so I told them I was a single tattoo artist from Hoboken who sold Avon on the side.

They didn't believe me.

* * *

'Ok, then—I guess I'll have to try something else,' I thought, as Wendy came into the room.

"*There* you are," she said, "I've been looking all over for you!

How's your period?" she asked in a loud voice.

"Mine's just fine," I said, in *another* loud voice. "How's yours?

Do you still have that big red stain on the back of your skirt?

I know you've got that pesky diarrhea too—how's that coming?"

* * *

Wendy's lips began to quiver, and her face blazed red, but that wasn't enough to stop me. I followed her out the door and waited until she got to the far end of hall.

"Hey, Wendy," I shouted after her.

"I hear you left a big mistake on your chair this morning.

I hope you can get more tampax before you make another. The janitors say they'll *never* get that nasty mess out of your chair."

Wendy growled something under her breath, made a quick turn to the right, and quickly disappeared around a corner.

What If He Forgets?

My husband came to visit every night
at 8:00, but one night he was late.
   'Oh, my God,' I panicked.
   'What if we're divorced?
   What if he's dead?
   What if he forgets my cigarettes?'

Group Therapy: Theater in the Round

Zip-A-Dee-Doo-Dah,
Zip-A-Dee-Day.
My, oh my, what a wonderful Day.
Plenty of sunshine headed my way.
Zip-A-Dee-Doo-Dah,
Zip-A-Dee-Day.

* * *

Phil sang out with gusto, as people came into the room and moved the chairs into a circle.

BB came in with Eileen Baker, a therapist from the addiction ward.

"Good morning everyone," he said.

"Morning," a few people mumbled.

* * *

"Well," BB said, "we always have a lot to talk about on Monday mornings, so let's get started.

Remember—everything we say is confidential. Nothing leaves this room.

* * *

Well, Phil," BB said, "you certainly sound lively today.

Did something happen over the weekend?"

"I don't know," Phil said.

"I don't remember."

"Did you see Dr. Thornton on Friday?"

"Yes, sir—I certainly did," Phil said, as he gave BB a salute.

"What did he say?"

"Nothing."

"*Really*, Phil?" BB asked. "He must've said *something*.

Did he adjust your medications?"

"Yeah—he increased the doses.

I don't see why he had to do that— I *told* him I've been feeling great, and now I'm telling you."

"That's *excellent*," BB said, "especially since you seemed so sad on Friday."

"Sad?"

"Yes. . .sad."

"Why do you say that?"

"Because—you talked about your mother for the first time.

Remember?"

Phil put his head between his hands and rubbed his temples.

"Oh, God" he moaned.

"What did I say?"

"You said the cancer has spread quickly, and she's already bedridden."

"Yeah—that's true," Phil said.

"But I'm not letting it bother me."

* * *

"You're *not?*" BB said.

"No."

"That's *remarkable*, Phil.

I think we should talk about that today."

"No," Phil said, "I'm not talking about it anymore.

* * *

Want to see something cool?" Phil asked, clearing his throat.

"Ok," everyone nodded.

He stood up and pulled his shirt over his chest. He turned in a circle so everyone could see.

It was a brand-new tattoo. A big red banner stretched all the way across his chest. There was something written inside. BB read it out loud:

"Go suck dead buffalo turds," it said.

Everybody stared at it, but nobody said a word.

* * *

"Is that *really* what you want to say to the world, Phil?" BB said.

"Yeah—why not?"

"Well, I admit it's short and sweet, but it certainly won't draw people to you."

"Good," Phil said.

"I hate it when people get all over me like a cheap suit."

"I'm surprised to hear you say that, Phil—you're always so friendly to everyone here."

"*No,* I'm not," Phil insisted, raising his voice.

"I don't *want* to be friendly."

"Are you sure, Phil?"

"Damn right I am."

"So be it," BB said, "but you're headed down a very lonely road."

"I *never* get lonely," Phil insisted, folding his arms across his chest.

* * *

"When do you see Dr. Thornton again?" BB asked.

"*I* don't know," Phil snapped.

"Why?"

"Well, I suggest you see him soon. You might want to tell him about your memory and your moods."

"Oh, I've already *told* him about *that*—that's all we ever talk about.

I'm *sick of it*."

* * *

"Well," BB said, "I really think Dr. Thornton can help."

"I don't," Phil said.

"Thornton's even crazier than me."

"What makes you say that?"

"Because—every time I try to talk to him, he just goes on and on about the self-help book he's writing. It's about survival skills. It's called

*Don't Get Caught with Your Drawers
Down.*

* * *

"*Really?*" BB said, as he scratched his chin.

"That's strange—I see Dr. Thornton every day, but he's never mentioned a book."

"That's because he's keeping it a secret," Phil said.

"He says if he lets it out before it's published, everyone will steal his ideas.

He only told *me* about it because *I'm* his favorite patient.

* * *

Anyway, it's like I told you, I've been feeling really great."

"Yes—you did say that, Phil."

"You think I'm lying?"

"No—not necessarily."

Phil looked BB in the eye.

"Well," he said, "I *am* feeling great.

That means I get to go home now.

Right?"

"No, not yet, Phil—you have to finish the ECT treatments first."

"ECT? What's that?"

"Electro-Convulsive Therapy," BB said.

"Oh, yeah—I remember now, but *I* don't need electricity anymore.

Now, take my roommate, Jason.

He needs it bad."

"We're not talking about Jason, Phil.

We're talking about you."

* * *

"Yeah—so?" Phil said, leaning forward in his chair.

"Listen, Doc—just give me a straight answer, ok?

When do I get out of here?"

"I already told you, Phil—we'll have to see how you feel after we finish the ECT."

* * *

Phil put his head between his hands and held it there for a minute.

BB thought he was falling asleep, but he suddenly broke into another song.

He belted this one out with a vengeance:

We gotta get out of this place.
If it's the last thing we ever do.
We gotta get out of this place.
Girl, it's the better life for me and you.

* * *

"Ok, Phil," BB said, "It's time to move on."

* * *

The room was silent for a few minutes, until Kenny blew his nose with a loud 'honk.'

"Beg your pardon, Kenny?" BB said.

"Oh, nothing."

* * *

"Ok—but tell me—is there something on your mind this morning?"

"Yes, actually," Kenny said, "there is one thing: I'm *really* sick."

"Sick? How so?"

"Well, you know they had to take my wisdom teeth out last month, and my

43

allergies have gone haywire—everything bothers me—from dander to dust.

Not only that—now I've got malaria."

"*Malaria?*" BB asked.

"Yeah—I've definitely got it."

"Really?" BB said, "how do you know?"

Oh, that's right—I forgot—you were in Afghanistan when you were in the army.

Right?"

"*No,*" Phil snapped. "I've never been in the army."

"Well then, what makes you think you've got malaria?"

"Listen, I've got a sore throat, a fever and chills, swollen glands, and a terrible cough.

I almost went to the hospital in an ambulance last night, but I fell asleep on the couch."

* * *

"Hold on, Kenny," BB interrupted.

"Let me ask you something."
"*What?*"

"How many times a day to you check yourself for lumps?"

Kenny blushed.

"Not that many," he said, lowering his voice.

"Right."

* * *

"Kenny? let me ask you a question."

"*What?*"

"Are your mother's parents still living?"

"Yeah—so?"

"So—how old is your grandfather?"

"Eighty."

"And your grandmother?"

"She's seventy-six."

"How about your father's parents?"

"Yeah, they're still alive. He's 78. She's 74."

* * *

"Well then," BB said. "sounds like you've got a great set of genes on both sides."

"Yeah—I guess so."

"Right—then why do you choose to worry yourself to death?"

* * *

Valerie sat very still as she stared at the floor.

"Are you ok?" Eileen asked.

"Yeah—I'm alright."

Valerie was a divorced mother of two who was working on her M.A. in urban planning.

Her ex-husband, Jackson, was a senior partner in the most prestigious law firm in Princeton.

* * *

Valerie and Jackson were happily married for three years—until he was diagnosed with testicular cancer.

The doctors moved quickly—they operated the day after they found the tumor.

Still, they had to remove one of Jackson's testicles to be sure they got all the cancer.

* * *

"*That's* when he started cheating," Valerie said.

"He thought I didn't know what he was up to, but I knew his every move.

* * *

I was completely devastated when I found out. I didn't eat or sleep for days, and I couldn't concentrate on anything.

It got so bad, I had to take a leave of absence from school.

I don't remember what I did during the leave, except I ate everything in sight and slept around the clock.

One day I realized that the marriage would always make me miserable. I cried about it for a long time, but then I realized what I had to do.

I filed for divorce.

I thought that would make it easier to deal with Jackson, but it just got worse.

* * *

He makes over $500,000 a year, but he's always late with alimony and child support.

I have to call him every month and remind him to send a check.

I just called his office the other day."

"Oh, I'm sorry, Valerie," his secretary, said, "Jackson's not in today."

"He went to a retirement party on Friday afternoon. It must've been a good one, because he never came back.

I was shocked when he called in this morning—he was in Paris!

He said he and a "special friend" were sitting in a café across the street from Notre Dame. They were making champagne toasts to the Almighty.

He *said* he'd be back by Friday, but I have my doubts."

* * *

"I hung up the phone, went to my computer, and wrote an email message."

'Dear Jackson,' it said.

'So glad to hear you went to Paris. Hope you had a ball.'

BB choked on his coffee, but nobody else made a sound.

* * *

Valerie suddenly felt light-headed. She leaned back in her chair and closed her eyes.

"What is it, Valerie?" BB asked.

"Oh, I don't know. I was just wondering if I really belong in here."

BB looked her straight in the eye.

"So was I," he said.

* * *

"Valerie?" Eileen said, "didn't you have a doctor's appointment on Friday?"

"Yes, I did."

"That's what I thought—how did it go?"

"Not very well."

"Oh, no—what happened?"

"The doctor said I need a new shunt," she said with a sigh.

"That means brain surgery all over again."

* * *

"What's a shunt?" Kenny asked.

"It's a drain that moves fluid from the brain down to the stomach,"

Valerie said, "where it can't do any harm."

* * *

"*Wow*," Kenny said, "What's wrong with your brain?"

"I have hydrocephalus."

"You have *what*?"

"Hydrocephalus," Valerie said.

"You probably know it as 'water on the brain.'

"Oh, man," Kenny said, "I've never heard of *that*. Sounds serious."

"It is," Valerie said.

Kenny took a close look at Valerie's head.

"Are you going to die?" he asked, eagerly.

"No," she said, "the shunt takes the pressure off the brain, so I'll be ok."

"Oh," Kenny said, as he leaned back in his chair, deflated.

"Well, does it hurt?"

"No, not really," Valerie said.

"Sometimes I get terrible headaches, but I have medication for that.

"I just get dizzy a lot, and I have trouble walking."

"Well then," Kenny said, "I must have that hydro-something too!"

I'm dizzy all the time, and I can hardly walk. There must be something wrong with *my* brain."

"*Oh, cut that out, Kenny,*" BB said.

"Your brain is just fine."

* * *

Roger suddenly snapped out of a daydream. He rubbed his eyes and sat up straight.

"Did I hear something about a shunt?"

"Yes, you did," Valerie said.

"Oh, *I* know all about shunts—they're for people with water on the brain.

Right?"

"Yes."

"There was a girl in my fourth-grade class who had that," Roger said.

"Her head looked like a big balloon. We used to call her 'bubble brain.'

He laughed.

* * *

"Tell me something, Roger," Valerie said.

"Have you always been an asshole?"

"What?" he said.

"I am *not* an asshole."

"Well you must have been one when you were in fourth-grade. Otherwise, you'd never have made fun of that poor little girl."

* * *

"Oh, *come on*," *Roger said.*

"We didn't mean anything by it.

It was just a joke."

"*You're* a joke," Valerie said, "a big, pathetic joke."

* * *

Roger jumped to his feet.

He looked down at BB.

"Are you going to let her talk to me like that?" he demanded.

"Roger," Eileen said softly, "I think you should step outside and take a break."

"Why don't you tell *her* to take a break?" he said, pointing at Valerie.

"Because—*she's* not angry."

* * *

"Ok—*that's* it," Roger said.
"I'm out of here."
"Wait!" Kenny said.
"You can't leave in the middle of a session."
"Oh, no?" Roger snapped.

"*Watch me.*"

* * *

Roger jumped up, pushing his chair over behind him. It landed with a loud clang.
"You know something?" he said.
"*You* people are all full of shit."
He marched out of the room, slamming the door behind him.

* * *

The room was silent for a few seconds, when an alarm suddenly went off with a high-pitched whine. It jolted everyone to attention.
"It's the fire alarm!" Kenny screamed.

"Alright people," BB said softly, "let's stay calm.

Just move *slowly* out to the hall and take the exit next to the stairs."

* * *

They met up in the courtyard outside the building just as the alarm stopped.

"Everybody ok?" BB asked.

They nodded.

"Well, that's the end of today's session. We'll pick up where we left off tomorrow."

It was lunch time, and everybody moved to the cafeteria.

* * *

BB was the only one who stopped to look around.

Roger was sitting on a bench across the yard.

He took a deep drag on his cigarette as he looked over at BB and mouthed a few words.

"Go suck dead buffalo turds," he said with a laugh.

It's Just Noise

I wandered around the halls one day—
just looking for something fun.

I gave up after an hour and threw
myself down on a couch in the lounge.

The air conditioners blasted at
full boom, and four huge TVs roared
down from the ceiling. Doctors,
nurses, aides and patients zig-zagged
around the room in different
directions.

The place was buzzing.

* * *

The woman sitting next to me looked
over with a grin.
    "When I get out of here," she said,
"I'm going to a heavy-metal marathon
at city stadium. Then I'm going
Christmas shopping at the mall. When
I'm done with that, I'm going to the
airport at rush hour—just to feel
like I belong."
    'Gee, she must be *awfully* smart,'
I thought. 'She knows that if you hold

on to your sense of humor, you don't
have to be so terrified all the time.

Father Knows Best

Marty offered Buddy an outstretched hand.

"Hi—Marcus Sinclaire here—but you can call me Marty.

You're Buddy Evans. Am I right?"

"Yeah," Buddy said with a note of weariness. He really didn't feel like talking, but he forced himself to speak.

They were sitting opposite each other at a table in the cafeteria.

* * *

"Who are you?" Buddy asked abruptly, as his right eye began to twitch.

"I'm a friend of your father's," Marty said.

"We work together in the home office."

"Oh, yeah—I remember you now—you came to a couple of softball games last year."

"That's right," Marcus said. "That was me."

"Anyway, your father asked me to stop by—just to make sure you're ok.

He's really worried about you."

"I *bet* he is."

* * *

It was hard to tell Marty's age, but he looked about fifty. So far, he wore it pretty well, though he had the beginnings of a bald spot and a slight pot belly.

Marty always wore a suit, but it often had frayed cuffs and broken hems. His shirts and ties should never have been in the same room, much less on the same person.

To make matters worse, Marty's breath smelled of stale cigarettes and bad breath mints, and his body let off waves of a sweet, spicy cologne.

The combination was enough to debilitate anyone within 50 yards.

* * *

Buddy was over 6'0" tall, and he weighed 165 pounds. His body was lean and fluid. His face was angular and handsome, but it was covered with cuts and bruises.

He had a sling on his right arm and a cast on his left leg.

* * *

Marty looked Buddy up and down.

"Man, you look like you've been through the ringer, son.

What the hell happened?"

Buddy grimaced at his cup of coffee.

"I had an argument with my father," he said. "Then I got hit by a car."

"Wow," Marty said, "I thought *I'd* been through some rough times with *my* father, but it was never as bad as all that."

* * *

"It wasn't that bad between us either," Buddy said, "until the other night.

I was having dinner with my parents, and things were going great—until my father said I should drop out of school and get a job.

I said it was a bad idea, but he told me to get off my lazy ass and start making some money for a change. He went on and on about it, raising his voice and pounding his fist on the table.

I just couldn't stand it anymore.

I ran upstairs and got his gun."

* * *

"Oh no," Marty said.

"Oh yes—I went back down to the dining room and put the gun inside his ear.

'Why can't you listen to me anymore?' I asked.

"Oh, my God," Marty said.

"Yeah—it turned into a real circus. My sisters started screaming, and my mother got down on her knees to pray. My father told them to shut the hell up, but they just kept going.

I saw my brother sneak into the kitchen. He picked up the phone and made a call. I knew he was talking to the police.

I had to get the hell out of there.

* * *

I ran out into the street and just kept going as fast as I could. I was halfway across town before I finally stopped to catch my breath.

I tried to keep going, but a huge cramp hit me in my side. It hurt so bad I had to lie down right there on the pavement. I just couldn't move anymore.

A car came screeching around the corner. It was headed straight at me, and it was going way too fast to stop.

I knew I was going to get hit.

I froze.

* * *

I don't remember anything after that. All I know is I woke up in this godforsaken place.

That was three days ago, and I'm *still* trying to get the hell out of here."

* * *

"Wow," Marty said, "you must have been pretty worked up—to put a gun to your father's head like that."

"Oh, no—that wasn't me," Buddy said. "That was Freddie Payne."

"Freddie Payne? Who's Freddie Payne?"

Buddy looked at Marty in surprise.

"You don't know Freddie Payne? *Everybody* knows Freddie."

Marty gave him a blank stare.

"Anyway," Buddy said, "Freddie's a good friend of mine.

He's usually pretty cool, but sometimes he thinks he's Harry Callahan, and he acts out all over the place.

Truth is, he's a nice guy, but he's stone-cold crazy."

* * *

"Listen, if you run into Freddie, don't tell him I said that, ok?"

Marty pulled out a handkerchief and blew his nose.

"Don't worry, kid—I won't say a word."

* * *

"So," Marty said, "you should be getting out of here soon. . .right?"

"That's what I want to know," Buddy said. They keep telling me I can go home tomorrow, but when the time comes, they say I'm not ready."

* * *

Buddy took a close look at Marty.

"Think you can get me out of here?"

"I don't know, Buddy. It looks like a tough situation, but I'll talk to your father. He knows everybody in this town. He must be able to do *something*."

Buddy put his head between his hands and rubbed his temples.

"My *fucking* father," he said.

* * *

"Try not to blame him, son—he just can't stop worrying about you."

"Really? Buddy said, "He *ought* to be worried about himself."

"What do you mean?"

Buddy sighed.

"I don't know—there's something wrong with him—he's been acting strange for months now."

"Strange—how?" Marty asked.

"Oh, I don't know—we used to go camping and hiking every year. We even went to Disney World and the Grand Canyon.

We had so much fun back then, but my father can't laugh at anything anymore."

* * *

"Well, he's been worried about you for a long time, son.

He said this is the fourth time you've broken a bone in the last six months."

"Yeah—so?"

Marty shifted his weight in his chair.

"Buddy, let me ask you something."

"Has anyone ever said you were accident prone?"

"No—not that I remember."

* * *

Buddy kept swinging his right foot back and forth as they talked—back and forth, back and forth.

He put his hand on his knee a few times, as if stop the motion, but it didn't work.

* * *

"Buddy, I have to ask you another question, but please don't take it the wrong way."

"Oh, *shit*," Buddy said, "what is it now?"

"Well, have you ever thought about life insurance?"

"Life insurance? No—why—should I?"

"Yes, you should—I mean God forbid, but what if you have another accident and things didn't turn out so well this time?"

Buddy frowned into his coffee.

* * *

"Trust me, Buddy—I'm here to help," Marty said.

"Everyone needs a little extra protection now and then.

* * *

Listen, I work for Mutual Life Indemnity, and we've got a policy that would be just right for you. It's called the Guaranteed Whole Life Plan.

It's perfect for people who are just starting out. It'll pay out $50,000 if, God forbid, something should happen to you."

"Well, maybe," Buddy said, "but can't we talk about it later?"

"Sure, kid.

* * *

Anyway, I hope they let you out of here soon," Marty said, "but in the meantime, don't you think it would be good to get some insurance going so you'll already be covered when you get home?"

"Yeah," Buddy said, "I guess you're right."

* * *

"Excellent," Marty said, as he quickly pulled a fist-full of forms from his briefcase and handed it to Buddy.

Buddy glanced at the forms, but he just squinted and bit his lip.

"I know Buddy," Marty said, "it looks like a lot of paperwork, but it's really not that bad. Just fill in what you can and give me your John Hancock on pages two and five. I'll do the rest.

I'll be back tomorrow to pick up the forms.

"Ok," Buddy said.

* * *

"Oh, wow," Marty said, glancing at his watch, "I've *got* to get back to the office.

Business is booming—we can hardly keep up."

He got up and headed for the door.

"You *are* coming back tomorrow?" Buddy asked. "Right?"

"Sure, kid—same time, same place."

* * *

"Oh, I almost forgot," Marty said, as he turned back to Buddy.

"I'll also need a check for $44.50 to cover the premium for the first month."

"Gee," Buddy said, "I don't know if I can swing that right now."

"Listen, kid, I know it may sound like a lot, but think about what you're getting for your money—$50,000 worth of protection!

Sure sounds like peace of mind to me."

* * *

Marty quickly set up a stack of brochures and business cards on the center table in the lounge.

"Listen, Buddy" he said, "tell your friends to take these—you might just be doing someone a big favor."

They headed down the hall to the elevator.

* * *

"My girlfriend wants to get married," Buddy said suddenly.

"Oh, no, Buddy. You've got to watch out for that type—they're *everywhere.*"

"Yeah, I guess so.

What about you, Marty? Are you married?"

"Oh, *brother,* am *I* ever married—I'm more married than anybody I know.

My wife's five months pregnant, and she's already enormous. She promises to lose the weight as soon as the baby's born, and I'll tell you what—

she'd *better* do it—and do it fast. My high school reunion's coming up in June, and I'm not going with a big, fat blimp on my arm."

* * *

Marty laughed as the elevator arrived. The doors opened and he stepped in.

Buddy reached out to shake his hand.

"See you tomorrow—*right Marty?*"

"Sure, kid. I'll be here."

* * *

A nurse waved at Buddy as he walked back onto the ward.

"Hey Gina, he said, "guess what?"

"What's that, Buddy?"

"I just met a guy named Marty. He's going to be my best friend!"

"That's great, Buddy!"

"Yeah, he was here for over an hour today, and he's coming back tomorrow."

* * *

Marty was headed for his car when he realized he forgot his sunglasses.

He walked back into the lounge, as one of the nurses said, "I saw your brochures on the table—sounds like your work is really important."

"Yeah, well—it's important to help people out these days—especially people like these."

"People like what?"

"Oh, you know—people with... problems."

"Problems?"

"Well, I don't know—aren't they all retarded or something?

I mean they sure *look* retarded."

* * *

The nurse gathered up the brochures and business cards as soon as Marty left.

She handed them to an aide.

"Here," she said, "get rid of these."

Marty and Buddy huddled over coffee in the cafeteria the next morning.

"You know you can name anyone you want as beneficiary," Marty said.

"What's a beneficiary?"

"That's the person who gets the $50,000 if, God forbid, something should happen to you."

"Wow, that's a lot of money," Buddy said.

"I bet you could buy a new truck with that."

"Oh, you could buy one hell of a new truck."

* * *

"So," Marty said, "who will you name as beneficiary—your father—right?"

"Oh, God no, not *him*."

"Why not?"

"Because—he likes everybody else better than me—even his dog."

"Oh, come on kid—I know you're just joking."

"No—I'm not—but it's alright—*I* like his dog better than him, too."

* * *

"Wouldn't you like to leave the money to *someone*?" Marty asked.

"Your girlfriend maybe?"

"No, not *her*. I caught her cheating on me last month."

"Oh, man, I'm telling you, Buddy—they're *all* like that."

"Well, I really thought I could forgive her at first, but I'm not so sure now. I keep thinking about this other girl in my math class. She's really hot, and she keeps giving me sexy looks.

I think she wants to be friends—or maybe more."

"You go Buddy—sounds like you're one step ahead of her!"

* * *

"Listen, Buddy, we can't turn in this paperwork without naming a beneficiary.

Can't you think of anyone else?"

Buddy leaned back in his chair, put his hands behind his head, and looked up at the ceiling.

"Let's see," he said, swiveling around in circles.

He stopped suddenly and sat up straight.

"*I know,*" he said, "I'll leave it to Izzy."

"Izzy? Oh, great.

Let me guess—Izzy's another girlfriend. Right?"

"Oh, no—Izzie's my dog."

* * *

"Your dog?"

"Yes, but she's really more than that—my mom says she's my soul mate."

Marty used his pencil to scratch the back of his head.

"Are you *sure* there's no one else, Buddy?"

"I'm sure—it's got to be Izzy."

"Ok, Buddy—it's your money, and I'll be glad to take it from you."

Buddy looked at him in surprise.

"Oh, don't worry kid," Marty laughed, "I was just kidding."

* * *

"Ok, Marty—but do you *really* think I need all this insurance?"

"Of course, you do, son. I mean what if, God forbid, you have another accident?"

"Ok," Buddy moaned, "what is it this time?"

"Well, let's just say you go mountain climbing and you slip and fall off a cliff."
"Mountain climbing?"

"Sure—why not?"

"Ok, if you say so," Buddy said, "but let me ask you something."

"Yes?"

"Am I hurt?"

"Well, yes, Buddy—I'm afraid you are."

"Is it bad?"

"Yes—it's very bad."

"Alright," Buddy said slowly.

"Am I dead?"

Marty looked down at the floor, his left eye twitched as he cleared his throat.

"Yes, Buddy. I'm afraid you are."

Buddy paused and bit his lip.

"Oh wow," he said suddenly. That's really great! I've always wanted to be dead."

Almond Joy

October 6, 1991

Dear Eddie,

Listen—I have something important to tell you: I started thinking about chocolate three days ago, and now I can't stop.

I'm pretty good about resisting it during the day, but the nights are rough.

I went on a search at 2:00 this morning, but I couldn't even find an ounce.

My roommate has been sympathetic. She told me about a secret candy machine in the back of a closet behind the lounge. I quickly tracked it down.

I found a miracle in that machine. It was sitting right there under the glass—an Almond Joy bar.

My hands trembled as I opened the wrapper.

I was savoring the first bite when I spotted a stack of post cards on top of the candy machine.

* * *

"Hey," I said to an aide, "are these for us?"

"Yeah," he said, "we put them out so patients can write to family and friends, but nobody ever uses them. They just sit here collecting dust. Take as many as you want—they're on the house."

The post cards had a little sketch of the hospital on the top. Beneath that it said, *Harmony House—the perfect place for peace of mind.*

* * *

I grabbed a handful of the cards, took a seat in the cafeteria, and addressed one to a friend.

"Having a wonderful time," I wrote,

"Wish you were here—not me.

* * *

Seriously though, "I wrote, "things are kinda quiet around here. There are only four other patients on my ward, but the marketing-types are trying to drum up new business all the time.

Anyway, I told my doctor about your special relationship with that ventriloquist's doll. That was enough for him. He wants you to catch the next bus down here and check yourself in.

Listen, don't worry—this place isn't so bad. Ok, so the food sucks, but the people are full of laughs—at least on good days.

I'm sure you'll fit right in.

There's just one little snag— they'll have to do a background check before they let you in. I hope that stuff about the belly dancer and the pawn shop doesn't come up—it makes you sound sort of...well...iffy."

Anyway, I highly recommend this place, especially since I found the Almond Joys.

Very truly yours,

Miss Whitney

Medications

The nurses made us get into a long line every time we took our meds.

We all had to tell them exactly what we were on before they handed over the pills.

I was on Nardil, Wellbutrin, Cogentin, Lamictal and Geodon.

For some reason, I couldn't remember the Cogentin. They made me repeat it one or two times before they finally gave it to me.

* * *

They watched closely as we swallowed every single pill.

Allergies

My husband's eyes welled up with tears one night as he was leaving, but he tried to hide them under his allergies.

"Don't worry," I said, rubbing the back of his neck.

"The dog will cuddle up with you when you get home."

It's All in the Cards

I was really surprised when BB showed up at my door the other day.

He came in and looked around the room.

"Good morning, madam," he said.

"Yeah, sure."

The sight of him standing in my little cubby-hole made me nervous.

'It must be weird to be a shrink,' I thought, 'making people uneasy everywhere you go.'

* * *

BB picked up a pile of cards from the bureau.

"What's all this?" he said.

"Oh, it's just a bunch of get well cards."

"Really? Who sent them?"

"Friends."

"Oh—friends—how nice."

"Yeah. I guess so."

"You *guess* so?" he said.

"Do you mean to tell me all these people went out of their way just to send you a card?"

"Yeah," I said, biting my lip.

"Then why have you left them in this messy pile?"

"I don't know," I said, "what am I supposed to do with them?"

"Why not stand them up on the bureau so people can see you have a lot of friends who care about you?"

"Yeah—I guess I could."

"Well," he said, "I'm very glad to hear that—there might just be hope for you yet."

* * *

"Good day, madam," he said as he turned to leave.

* * *

I took a peek into the hall to make sure he was gone. Then I stood the cards up in a neat little circle.

Elementary, My Dear Watson

I was just coming out of the chapel last night when I saw a group of people huddled in a circle outside the cafeteria.

They were looking at something on the floor, but I was too far away to see what it was.

I went to get Alison, my next-door-neighbor and partner-in-crime.

* * *

Alison had been in the place for over three months—longer than anybody else.

She had a terrible lisp, which made her self-conscious, so she only spoke when she had no choice.

Some people took Alison's silence as arrogance, but I'd spent some time with her—time enough to know she could be really warm and friendly.

* * *

I told Alison about the crowd outside the cafeteria.

"I'm going down there to check them out," I said.

"Ooh, take me with you," she giggled with a spark in her eye.

Alison loved it when we got up to no good.

"I want to see if I can find Kurt," she said, "that cheap-ass fool. He lost my last dollar in the coke machine last night, and he's been hiding from me ever since."

"Well then," I said, "let's go get *his* last dollar."

* * *

We headed down the hall, but by the time we got to the cafeteria, the crowd had moved to the lounge.

I *hated* the lounge. It was always full of toxic gossip and Neanderthal fights, but we heard something different last night.

"Aww," people sighed as we went in. That's when I caught a glimpse of her.

* * *

She was a big, beautiful dog—solid black with one bold white stripe that started at the back of her neck, ran all the way over her head, and ended at the tip of her nose.

"Her name is Watson," said Donna, a nurse from the second floor.

* * *

Donna gave Watson a pat on the head.

"She's been with me since she was a puppy."

"That's wonderful," I said, "but how did she get a name like Watson?"

"Oh, I don't know—I really liked the name, and it just seemed to suit her. Besides, she doesn't care if her name was meant for a boy.

* * *

Donna made coffee while Watson worked the room. She moved from one person to the next, giving big, sloppy kisses to everyone, and getting the same in return.

* * *

An older woman suddenly floated into the room. She was wearing a gigantic red caftan and yellow fuzzy slippers.

"Watch this," she giggled, stretching out her arms so her sleeves flowed around her like a big pair of wings.

She made the sound of an airplane coming in low as she circled the room.

She dive-bombed two patients and barely missed a nurse.

"*Eureka!*" she yelled.

"I *told* them I could fly, but they didn't believe me."

"They never will," said a young man from the back of the room.

"Hi," she said, as she came in for a landing.

"My name's Rebecca," she smiled, "but you can call me Lindy."

* * *

"Fine by me," he said, "Lindy it is."

"I'm Austin," he said, pointing to his chest.

"Want to have sex?" he asked, shifting his weight from one foot to the other.

"Not right now," Lindy said, "maybe later."

* * *

"*I'm* bipolar with a touch of paranoia," she smiled, as she pulled on her hair.

"*So?*" Austin said.

"*I've* got multiple personalities.

I bet you can't guess who I am now."

"Oh, I don't know," Lindy laughed.

"Wait—don't tell me—let me guess.

Oh—I know—you're Paul Revere," she said, "warning the good guys that the bad guys are coming.

Right?"

"No," Austin said, "I'm F. Lee Bailey—I'm getting ready to plead my case."

* * *

"Lindy," the nurse yelled from the back of the room.

"Didn't I tell you last night—you're not allowed to fly in here.

If you don't stop, you'll have to go back to your room."

* * *

Lindy lowered her head and slumped her shoulders.

"Aww, *shit*," she said, "this place is no fun.

I want to go home."

* * *

Another woman came in just then. She sauntered around the room for a few minutes and stopped to make an announcement.

"I'm Audrey," she said, as she cleared her throat.

"Know what?" she asked the room.

"I came in here to tell you all something," she said. "This place doesn't need more doctors or nurses. What it *really* needs is a decent water fountain.

That thing down the hall just spits in your face when you try to get a drink," she said, licking her lips.

* * *

The man sitting next to me tapped me on the shoulder and smiled.

"Lithium," he said, nodding at Lindy, "it'll suck so much water out of you, you'll feel like a prune."

* * *

Audrey looked around the room with a grin.

"Well, folks," she said, "I've got to get going—I need more H_2O."

She blew a big kiss to the room, as she backed out the door.

* * *

"I'm surprised they let Watson in here," I said to Donna as she plopped down in the chair next to me.

"Yeah, well" she said, "they finally figured out that pets make people feel good, so they're letting them visit hospitals and nursing homes.

"They should've done that a long time ago," I said.

"Amen."

* * *

An aide dimmed the lights, put a movie in the DVD player, and hit 'play.'

Everyone seemed to relax a little, as the Marx Brothers came to life on the tube.

Watson took a place at Alison's feet, but Alison ignored her.

* * *

It was almost ten o'clock when the movie ended. Donna glanced at her watch and stood up quickly.

"Wow," she said, "I didn't know it was so late. I've *got* to get home."

She gathered her things and headed for the door, but she suddenly realized something was missing.

It was Watson.

Donna called her name, but Watson didn't come.

A panic rose on her face, but she tried to force a smile, as she motioned to me.

"We've got to search the place," she whispered.

* * *

It only took a few minutes to check the office and kitchen, but there was no sign of Watson.

The lounge would take longer—it was a huge room crammed full of old game tables, broken exercise equipment, and miss-matched furniture.

* * *

We searched for over half-an-hour.

We were just about to give up when I spotted Alison across the room. She was sound asleep in a big easy chair with Watson draped across her lap.

As I came closer, I thought I heard her mumble something, but then I realized she was singing.

Her voice was soft, but I caught the words:

He's got the whole world in his hands.

He's got the whole world in his hands.

He's got you and me, brother, in his hands.

He's got you and me, sister, in his hands.

He's got the whole world in his hands.

* * *

Watson was lost in a deep sleep with her head nuzzled under Alison's chin. They took deep breaths in unison—a snore every time they took in air, a whistle every time they let it out.

* * *

The room was calm and peaceful—until I tripped on Alison's chair as I went to get coffee.

She bolted up and looked around.

"What the hell?" she yelled.

"What's going on?"

"Oh, nothing," I whispered.

"You and Watson just took a little nap."

"Oh—who the hell is Watson?"

"*That's* Watson," I said, pointing to her on the floor.

"The two of you made a perfect pair—all cuddled up in that big chair. She was kissing you on the face."

"Oh, no," Alison groaned.

"Oh, yes," I said, "and you looked like you loved it—you even smiled once. At least it *looked* like a smile from here."

* * *

Alison looked down at Watson.

"That's *disgusting*," she said, wiping her face on the sleeve of her shirt.

She closed her eyes and went back to sleep.

* * *

"It's funny," she said, as we walked back to my room that night.

"I could have sworn I *hated* dogs. I can't believe I let one get so close. I guess I just forgot."

She paused for a minute and cleared her throat.

"The doctor told me I'd forget a few things after ECT," she said, "but I thought he was just kidding."

* * *

"My husband is coming to visit tomorrow night," she said suddenly.

"Oh, that'll be nice."

"I hope so, but I'm really worried."

"Worried? Why?"

"Because," she said, "my family says my husband and I have a great relationship, but I can't even remember getting married."

Wardrobe Dilemma

There was a new woman in the lounge today. She sat on a table, kicking her legs back and forth as she talked.

Back and forth. Back and forth.

To make matters worse, she was wearing about a dozen of those bangle bracelets, and they made a horrible racket every time she kicked.

* * *

"What day is it?" she said.
One person thought it was Wednesday, but two insisted on Thursday.

"No—wait," she said quickly, "I just had my nails done yesterday, so it must be Thursday.

Thursday?" she yelped in surprise.

"Do you know what I thought I'd do on Thursday?
I thought I'd go shopping at Bloomies, get my hair done at Sylvia's

Salon, and then meet the girls for lunch."

She looked around the room in mock horror.

"So, who knew?" she said.

* * *

She was just sinking back in her chair with an exasperated sigh when a nurse stuck her head in the door.

"Is there a Fanny here?"

"That's me," the woman said, as she stood up to leave.

"Gee, folks," she said, "it's been a pleasure to meet you."

She paused for a moment.

"I can't *believe* it—all this happened so fast," she said.

"I didn't even get a chance to plan my wardrobe.

What do you wear for something like this?"

Office Visits

The people from my office visited as a strange little team.

They crept into my room, slowly looked around, and approached me with caution.

* * *

Well, you *look* ok," my boss said, eyeing me up and down.

"Oh, yeah," his secretary said.

"You look just like the *old* Whitney.

Err, I mean you *used* to look great every day, but lately...she wrenched her hands.

Oh, *never* mind," she said, "just forget it."

* * *

The room fell into an awkward silence, but my supervisor broke it.

"You should be ok now," she said.

"Just make sure you take your medications every day."

She waved a finger in my face.

"God forbid you should go *bonkers* on us again."

* * *

They made small talk about the Christmas party, until they began to get restless. Then they said they had to go to a meeting back at the office.
They went out as carefully as they came in.

* * *

"What are they so nervous about?" I asked my husband when they were gone.

"*I* don't know," he snapped.

"Let's go get a coke."

Bet Your Bottom Dollar

I wandered into the lounge one afternoon as that game show, *Bet Your Bottom Dollar,* came blaring out of three TVs.

I *hate* the guy on that show—what's his name—Gary something?

Anyway, he acts so sweet and innocent, but I say there's something sinister about him.

My girlfriend, Mertha, was going to see his show while she was on vacation in California last year, but I told her he was a serial killer. (I figured everybody needs a good travel agent. Right?)

Anyway, Mertha pretended she didn't care, but her daughter told me they went to see *The Price is Right* instead.

ECT

We had thunderstorms off and on for three days straight. The place felt dark and dreadful.

I sat in the auditorium by myself for a long time. Then I moved to the cafeteria and sat by myself there.

* * *

"You don't look good," BB said, scratching his chin.
"So? You don't so look good either."

"Let's just hold off on the sarcasm. Shall we?"

"Oh, gee—and I was just beginning to have some fun."
BB grimaced and cleared his throat.
"Ok, ok," I said. "What do you want to talk about today?"

* * *

"Well," BB said, leaning back in his chair, "*I* think ECT is in order now."

"ECT?"

"Electro-Convulsive Therapy."

"Oh my God—you mean like in the movies—where they put those plugs all over your head, connect you to a machine, and shoot electricity through your brain?"

"Yes, but—"
"Good *God*," I said, "you *still* do that!"
"We do—it can be very helpful for people who are severely depressed, and it's totally painless.
I think it's the best option for us now."

* * *

'Who was this mysterious 'us' he was suddenly talking about?' I thought. 'Was *he* going to hop up on a table and let somebody blast his brain into electrical oblivion?
Sounds good to me,' I thought.
'He can go first.'

* * *

"Hold on," I said, "it's one thing to say I was messed up by the time I was in third-grade, but send my brain into convulsions?

You must be joking."

I slammed my hand down on the edge of the table until a big, blue lump appeared on my knuckles. It hurt like hell, but I wasn't about to admit it.

Anyway, we haggled about ECT for about half-an-hour, but neither one of us was listening.

We finally agreed to bring my husband in for the next session.

* * *

I'm still not sure how they did it, but somehow the two of them convinced me to watch a film about ECT.

It explained the procedure step-by-step, and people talked about how it helped them climb out of depression.

When the film was over, BB turned to me.

"Any questions?" he asked.

"Yeah—plenty."

"Do I have to flail around like a rag doll and drool all over myself while all those people watch?"

"Don't worry," he said.

"There won't be a lot of people there, and the ones that are will be too busy doing their jobs to watch what you're doing."

"Oh yeah?" I said.

"Well, let's just say something goes wrong—can I sue you for a lot of money?"

"Of course, you can," he said, "but I think you're going to feel much better—even after just one treatment."

"Oh, sure," I said, rolling my eyes.

"Really," he said, "I've seen it happen before."

* * *

He almost smiled.

That worried me—BB was usually a sarcastic curmudgeon, but he sounded almost upbeat now.

'What's he so happy about?' I wondered.

"Listen," I said, "you know optimists annoy the hell out of me, so don't go getting cheerful on me all of a sudden."

"It doesn't become you."

* * *

Anyway, he and my husband went on for twenty minutes about the wonderfulness of ECT.

I tried to block them out.

* * *

I was stunned when I heard myself agree to the ECT a few minutes later. I still don't know why I did it, but I had to do *something* to make them stop talking.

'Oh, well,' I thought, 'if I let them do it, maybe they'll let me out of here.'

CAT Scan

They had to do a CAT scan of my brain before they started the ECT.

I was convinced they'd find something wrong.

I felt like Woody Allen—fretting about his brain tumor, but at least Woody could go home after they broke the bad news.

I'd have to go back to my room in the psych hospital.

* * *

Anyway, turns out they had to take me to a regular hospital to do the scan, and they were worried about how I'd react to the change of scenery.

Would I freak out and lose control in public? That would make them look pretty bad, so they worried some more.

* * *

They finally decided to send four aides to the hospital with me.

They surrounded me—two on each side—as we walked into the hospital and headed for the lab.

I felt like an inmate being escorted to the electric chamber by the prison guards.

* * *

Anyway, we made it to the lab.

They took me in right away and quickly did the scan.

"*See* that you guys?" I yelled at the aides when it was over, "I *told* you I wasn't crazy anymore."

They hurried me along, as we went back to the car.

The First Treatment: Pleading with my Sister

They strapped me down to an operating table, gave me an injection, hooked me up to an IV, and plastered rubber plugs all over my head.

I tried to scream, but they put a rubber guard inside my mouth.

* * *

I closed my eyes and drifted off to la la land.

* * *

I suddenly saw my baby sister. She was waving at me from across the room.

I'd already told BB how much I loved her, but she'd stopped speaking to me six years ago.

She was a radical lesbian feminist, and she thought I was too "conservative" because I was married to a man and lived in suburbia.

Anyway, the whole time I was under, I kept calling out to her—

"Eileen," I pleaded, "I love you more than my next breath. Will I ever see you again?"

I was crying when I woke up, and I couldn't stop.

* * *

Two men were talking off in the distance. They were speaking very softly, but I heard every word.

"Listen," a man said to BB, "I gave her as much valium as I could, but it just didn't take. I couldn't give her anymore."

"If she was upset when she woke up," BB said, "she didn't get enough.

Give her more next time."

The Second Treatment: The Jewish Leprechaun

'This is going to be a breeze—you won't feel a thing.'

That's what I told myself, as they hooked me up to the IV again.

They'd adjusted the valium, and I slipped back to la la land without a hitch.

* * *

I was in third grade again. It was 1961.

My teacher went around the room and asked everybody to tell the class about their religion.

Most kids said they were either catholic or protestant, but I just clutched.

I didn't know *what* I was.

I became more and more nervous as the question came close.

I felt sweaty and short of breath, but then I realized they wouldn't have

time to get to me. I was off the hook—
at least until tomorrow.

* * *

"What *are* we anyway," I asked my
father that night.

"I know you call mom the Jewish
leprechaun. Can't I just say that?"

"No," he laughed, "I don't think
that'll work."

I let out a long, frustrated sigh.

* * *

"Don't worry," he said, "just tell
them you're Unitarian. They won't ask
any questions."

"Ok, but what are we *really?*

Don't we have a religion—like
everybody else?"

My father went into his office and
came back a few minutes later with a
little silver box.

"Here," he said.

"I've been saving this for you for a long time.

I have one for your sisters too, but I don't think they're ready for it yet."

* * *

"Wow," I said, "what is it?"

"It's the answer to your question," he said, as he handed me the box.

I tore it open and pulled out a long silver pendant.

"It's *beautiful!*" I cried, as I put it around my neck and held it in my hands.

"What does it mean?"

"Take a close look," he said.

* * *

"See—there's a cross on one side—that's for the Christians.

There's a Star of David on the other side—that's for the Jews."

* * *

"Well, which side *am* I?" I asked impatiently.

"Listen," he said with a smile, "both sides are beautiful, and so are you."

Treatments Three through Eight

They shot electricity through my brain six times again over the next two weeks.

'Is this a reasonable thing?' I wondered, as I roamed around the halls, searching for my room.

* * *

I was still feeling a little iffy a few days later. I tried to watch everything carefully and concentrate, but everything was happening in the middle, and I was on the outskirts.

The Big Test: Can You Do Your Laundry?

I pulled my dirty clothes together one morning and went to the nurse's station.

The nurse was on the phone, so I put the clothes up on the counter.

I shifted my weight from one foot to the other and coughed a couple times.

She finally finished her call.

* * *

"Ok," she said, "what's all this?"

"I'm glad you asked," I said.

"*This* is my laundry. I've *got* to get it clean."

She nodded to an aide who walked me down the hall and pointed to a room full of washers and dryers.

"Here," she said, "you can wash your things in there."

* * *

The laundry detergent was in a vending machine, but I didn't have any quarters. I took a few dollar bills out of my pocket and went back to the aide.

"Can you change these for me?" I asked.

"We ran out of quarters an hour ago," she shrugged, turning back to her book.

*   *   *

I traced my steps back to my room and felt around in the 'secret' compartment inside my purse.

I was searching for quarters, but I came up with my wedding ring instead. (People were stealing things all over the place—wallets were missing, cash was gone, even clothes disappeared. Of course, *I* knew the nurses were guilty, but nobody else had figured that out.)

Anyway, as soon as I heard things were disappearing, I put my ring in the secret compartment and slept with my purse under my head.

*   *   *

I finally found some quarters and tried to make my way back to the laundry room. I got lost and had to ask for directions.

Anyway, all the washers were going full blast—except one. It was way in the back of the room, and I had to work my way around two big dryers to get to it.

That's when I noticed the little sign taped to the door of the washer.

'Out of Order,' it said, in neat little letters.

* * *

'They lie about every *fucking* thing around here,' I swore, as I trudged my way back to my room, leaving a trail of dirty underwear behind.

Tossing a Buick Across the Parking Lot

Two days after the ECT ended, I started fantasizing about a gigantic hot fudge sundae.

I was deep into the chocolate when an aide came over to give me my mail.

* * *

I wondered why I'd never noticed him before—he was a young black man who looked like he'd done some serious body building.

'I bet he could toss a Buick across the parking lot,' I thought, 'just to see where it would land.'

* * *

'Forget the Buick,' I told myself, as I admired his physique.

I hadn't felt sexually attracted to anyone in over six months. It made me tremble.

* * *

He walked over to me again.

'I don't *believe* it,' I thought, 'he must've read my mind!'

* * *

That's good—we can skip the boring preliminaries and get right down to business. We'll strip each other naked, fall down on that couch, and just *do it*—like a pair of bunny rabbits on a manic spree.

* * *

'Ut oh—here he comes,' I thought, as I bit my lip.

My palms were sweaty, and my mouth was dry.

I had to do *something* to keep myself under control, so I sent him another telepathic message.

'Ready and willing,' it said, 'no questions asked.'

* * *

I pretended I was caught up in my book as he came close.

"Sorry," he said, clearing his throat.

"I forgot to give you this," he said, handing me a package.

The tension was becoming unbearable.

I *had* to throw something, so I aimed the package at the chair next to me.

It landed with a thud.

He smiled.

* * *

I suddenly had the strongest urge to kiss him on the lips. I couldn't get away with that, so I forced myself to speak.

* * *

"What's it like," I said, "working in a place like this?"

"Oh, it's pretty interesting," he said, with a faint smile.

'*Shit*,' I thought, 'we'll never get anywhere if he keeps talking like that—he sounds like a diplomat—charming but cautious.'

* * *

"It must be hard," I said, "spending so much time with people who are sick. Think it's catchy?"

"Nah," he laughed, "I've been here for six months, and so far, so good."

"How about you—you feeling ok?"

"Yes," I said, "I'm ok *now*, but I was in pretty bad shape when I first got here—they had to lock me up in that *quiet area*."

"Oh, now *that's* a bad place to be," he said, "but I'm sure you caught on pretty fast—people do the strangest things around here all the time. They either laugh or cry, fight or faint, and they backstab each other every time they get the chance."

"I know," I said, "I've seen it myself.

That's why I can't sleep."

* * *

"Oh well," I laughed.
"Who needs sleep anyway?"

I leaned back in my chair and crossed my legs. My skirt slid up over my knees, and I didn't stop it.

* * *

"Is it ok if I ask you a question?" I said, trying to sound relaxed and friendly.

"Sure," he said, as he gave me a wink.

* * *

"Well—I just wondered—how do you maintain your sanity when you work in a place like this?"

"Oh, I *couldn't* maintain it for the first few weeks" he said.

I was nervous every morning and nasty every night.

My family worried.

But the secret came to me during visiting hours one night, when I saw a patient slap her mother across the face."

* * *

"Oh my God," I said, "that's outrageous."

"Not in this place it isn't. *Nothing's* outrageous here."

* * *

"Just a second," I said, as he was about to leave.

"Did you say something about a secret?"

"Yes—I did."

"Oh—*please*—tell me about it!"

"Well," he said, "turns out it's pretty simple.

If you *have* to be around broken people every day, take a step back and pretend it doesn't hurt."

Jigsaw Puzzle

I spotted an old jigsaw puzzle in the back of the lounge one night. I emptied the box and spread the pieces across a table. I was sorting them out when she crept up from behind.

She was wearing a big orange sweater, powder blue stretch pants, and neon yellow gloves with the fingers cut out.

* * *

She sat down opposite me, picked up a few pieces, and began to work the puzzle.

We worked on it for four nights straight, but she never said a word—not even her name.

'Maybe she just wants to remain anonymous while she's in here,' I thought.

'Why the hell didn't *I* think of that,' I wondered, as I looked down and realized my shoes didn't match.

* * *

I sat next to her in the cafeteria at lunch one day.

"Hi," I said, "I'm having pizza. How about you?"

"I don't eat," she snapped, shoving something into her pocket.

She stood up and left.

Speaking Up

I was really surprised when she spoke up in group one day.

"My mother murdered my sister and buried her in the woods," she said.

The room went completely silent—until a man cleared his throat.

"Did she get away with it?" he asked.

"Yeah—for a while. She told everybody my sister was away at summer camp and wouldn't be back until the fall.

* * *

That worked until mid-September, when my sister was supposed to come home.

My mother said she'd had a bad case of the flu. The couple who owned the camp invited her to stay on until she felt a little better, so she wouldn't be home for a while."

"What did people make of that?" the man asked.

"Oh, she had most of them convinced everything was fine, but she couldn't fool my grandmother or my aunt. They hadn't heard from my sister in weeks, and they knew something was wrong.

They just kept asking questions until they pieced it together."

"What did they do?" the man asked.

"They went to the police and turned her in.

The police started a big investigation. They came to the house and asked all sorts of questions.

I'm not sure what happened after that, but they put me in here a few weeks later."

* * *

"Have things been better for you since you've been here?" BB asked.

Her hands were trembling as she answered.

"No," she said, "they haven't, I just want to die."

She slid down further in her chair.

* * *

As the group broke up, I went over and tried to put my arms around her, but she just flinched when I came close.

"*Please* don't talk about yourself like that," I begged.

"Don't you know we love you?"

She put her head down on the table and waved me away.

* * *

They moved her into my room an hour later.

Rude Awakening

I woke up to a strange sound in the middle of the night.

It took my eyes a few seconds to adjust to the light, but there she was on the bed—jumping up and down on her stomach. She let out a loud grunt every time she hit the bed.

* * *

An aide suddenly yelled out from the hall.

"She's got something!"

Four of them rushed into the room. They turned her over, pulled something from her hands, and wrestled her away.

* * *

I lay there, silent and shaking, until one of the aides came back.
"You won't *believe* what she was doing," she said to the nurse.
"She was trying to stab herself in the chest with *this*," she said, holding up a fork.

"Oh, my God—did she really think that would work?"

"I guess so," the aide said.

They had a good laugh.

* * *

The next morning her bed was stripped, and her clothes were gone.

"Where is she?" I demanded.

"Oh, you mean *that* one," the nurse said, looking doubtfully at the empty bed.

"*That* one was *completely* nuts."

We had to transfer her out of here last night. We won't be seeing her again."

"*Bullshit*," I said.

"She'll be back."

Missing Person

I checked the cafeteria about a dozen times a day over the next week, but there was no sign of her.

* * *

I asked a nurse about her when I was discharged a week later.

"We don't have anything on her," she said.

"Are you sure? You *must* have *something.*"

"I don't think so—there's nothing here."

She turned back to her paperwork.

* * *

"Oh, wait," she called out as I was about to leave.

"I just found her file. It got stuck at the bottom of this pile."

She opened it and took a look.

"That's funny," she said, adjusting her glasses.

"The exit form usually shows where they went after discharge, but this just has a question mark next to 'destination.'

Epilogue: Struck by the Stigma, or Friendship is a Lost Art

Mindy Tyson was over 1,000 miles away when I had the nervous breakdown.

Mindy and I had been best friends ever since we were roommates in college. That was over thirty years ago, but we could still talk about anything—from flea market treasures, to career ambitions, to great music, to men.

* * *

Mindy was studying to become a veterinarian at a big university in upstate New York when I went into the hospital.

Now in her final year of school, she was under a lot of pressure. She had to finish her thesis and pass the Board exams, and she didn't have much time to do it.

* * *

I waited until Mindy came home before I told her about the breakdown.

She was awfully upset.

"But *why*," she cried, "*why* did you have to fall apart?

Now I can't even talk to my friends about you—how can I tell them what you've done?"

* * *

"Listen," I said, "let's make this a multiple-choice question. Ok?"

"Oh, alright," she sighed.

"Good, in that case, it goes like this:

I had a nervous breakdown because,

a) My husband was cheating;
b) My career was moving at a snail's pace;
c) I couldn't have a baby;
d) I messed up my latest paint-by-numbers masterpiece;
e) My mother died;
f) All of the above;
g) None of the above; or,
h) Some strange combination of the above, which messed with my mind.

"Wow," Mindy said, "you're talking way too fast—I can hardly keep up."

"Oh, that reminds me," I said, "we're almost out of coffee. I'll run over to *Caffeine City* this afternoon and get some of that mocha java blend.

Let's see, then I've got to stop at Sydney's Salon for a cut and curl, and I need some pantyhose. By the way, have you tried that new brand—the ones with the extra support?

No? Well, they feel great once you get them on, if you *can* get them on. Believe me, I know it's a struggle, but it's worth it—they'll make you look sleek and sexy.

Granted, you may feel a little cramped at first, but it's like my Aunt Gladys used to say, 'You have to suffer to be beautiful.'

Aunt Gladys was nobody's fool.

* * *

Anyway, then I've got to go to the dry cleaners to pick up my red dress for tomorrow night—the neighbors are throwing a big party to celebrate their son's graduation.

Oh, before I forget—I have to bake something for that party.

I was thinking about black forest cake, but I might just make a hazelnut torte instead.

What do you think, Mindy?

Mindy?

Oh, never mind," I said.

"I'll just pick up something at the bakery on the way home."

* * *

Mindy gave me her blank stare.

"Man, you're *still* talking too fast," she said.

"Can't you slow down?"

"Alright," I said.

I went to the bathroom and took three clonazepam—those pills the shrink told me to take if my mind started moving faster than my mouth.

* * *

Anyway, if you ask me, Mindy needed to put her sense of humor in gear. (I knew she had one, because she let it slip once in a while.)

Still, it often failed her when she needed it most—like when she accidentally locked herself in that port-a-potty at her son's first high school football game. It was just seconds before he scored *the* touchdown of the season, so she missed it.

Mindy could have used her sense of humor then, but she went home and wept for three days instead.

* * *

I took Mindy to the movies a lot, hoping she'd find something to laugh at, but she didn't like vaudeville or slapstick, and she *hated* situation comedies.

She usually complained about the 'God-awful' movie all the way home.

"*That* wasn't funny at all," she'd say. "Why'd you make me watch it?"

I hate to admit it, but sometimes I wanted to dump Mindy off at the next corner and keep on going.

Don't get me wrong—Mindy could be a loyal and loving friend, but everyone knew she was a test.

Most people just ignored her, but I refused to give up on Mindy. I knew she'd stick by me if I ever took myself too seriously.

* * *

I made a pitcher of iced tea and swept the front porch one afternoon, as I waited for Mindy to come over for lunch.

* * *

"Wow, you look *fantastic*," I said, as she got out of the car with her dog.

"Where'd you get those great jeans? They fit you like a glove. I've been looking all over for a pair like that, but I can't find them in my size.

Speaking of that, I've *got* to lose ten pounds before tomorrow night. I'd better have one of those diet thingies for lunch, and then fast until the party starts."

"You're ridiculous sometimes," she said.

"You know that?"

"Yes, I do—but at least I'm laughing."

"Go ahead," she said, "laugh yourself to death."

* * *

We went out to the backyard and settled into wicker chairs under a big elm tree. It was the first time we'd seen each other in over six months.

"Well," she said, "let me catch you up on the latest.

I finished up with a 4.8," she said quickly. It was the highest grade-point-average in the whole class.

Faculty said my thesis was brilliant, and I passed the Boards with flying colors."

She sat up straight and pulled her shoulders back, so her posture was perfect.

"*I'm* a full-fledged veterinarian now," she said.

* * *

"That's wonderful, Mindy. You did a great job."

"Yes—I did—didn't I?

And it's not just about school either," she went on.

"I also got a great job with the best vet practice in the state, and I started out at a *fabulous* salary.

I also found a *darling* little apartment in Princeton, bought a Mercedes, and got a complete makeover."

"*Wow,* girl—you've been busy! Did you really do all that in less than two months?"

"I sure did," she said.

"That's one thing I learned in school—I can do a lot of different things at the same time and still do a great job at all of them.

That's because I have an *incredible* attention span," she said, "and once I start a project, I don't stop until it's done."

"I know, Mindy," I said.

"I've seen you work like that before, and I'm glad you can get so much done, but *please* stop playing beat the clock—it'll kill you if you let it."

* * *

We sipped iced tea and munched on chips and salsa as we sat in the shade.

* * *

"So," I said, "when did you start the job?"

"Two weeks ago."

"Great," I said. "How do you like it so far?"

"Oh, no," she suddenly said, as she jumped up and chased her dog across the yard.

She pulled a scarf from his mouth with a sharp jerk.

"Harvey!" she screamed.

"I've *told* you a hundred times," she said, waving a finger in his face.

"Stop taking my things, and *don't* trample on the lawn—you'll ruin the grass.

Now go lie down under that tree."

Harvey crouched down close to the ground, as if he'd been struck on the head by something hard.

He did as he was told.

* * *

"It's a good thing he's so cute," Mindy said, tying Harvey's leash to the tree, "because sometimes I just want to take him to the nearest shelter and drop him off."

She carefully plucked the grass off her clothes, one blade at a time.

* * *

"So, how did it feel to have a *real* nervous breakdown?" she asked.

"Oh, it felt like being dragged down and swallowed up by quicksand—over and over again.

Just when I thought I was getting better, it sucked me right back down. I was beginning to think I'd *never* get out of that place.

Well, you can just imagine."

"Oh, no," she said, "*I* can't imagine."

"Nothing like that's ever happened in *my* family."

She sniffed.

* * *

"Oh, Mindy—I do love you, but try not to be such an asshole, ok?"

"I'm telling you the truth," she insisted.

"Everybody in my family is perfectly sane."

* * *

I knew she was fibbing then, because I remembered her grandmother—Helga.

Helga just barely escaped Nazi-occupied Poland in 1942, so you had to allow for her little idiosyncrasies.

Still, Helga thought she was back in Poland, and it made incredibly restless.

She often wandered around the neighborhood with her passport and her lucky penny stashed away in a secret pocket.

She spat a barrage of guttural Polish at anybody who got in her way. People couldn't tell exactly what she was saying, but they knew fighting words when they heard them.

* * *

I worried about Helga a lot.

Once I told Mindy about her outbursts.

"Oh, that's just Helga," she said.

"Nobody listens to her anymore—she's just a batty old lady.

Ignore her."

* * *

"So, Mindy," I said, "tell me about the job."

"Oh yeah," she said, "the practice is in one of the best neighborhoods in

Princeton. It sits in the middle of a quarter-acre of land, which we've turned it into a *magnificent* Japanese garden.

Anyway, now that I'm on board, we have six vets in all. That makes us the largest practice in the state.

Of course, all the other vets are raving about my work—they say they've never seen anyone so quick and careful.

Not only that, the clients are much more sophisticated than the ones I had at that horrible shelter in south Jersey.

Those people were all lower-income and—well—let's just face it—you get a better class of clients in Princeton."

"Oh, right," I said, pulling my sunglasses down from my forehead to cover my eyes.

* * *

"That's wonderful, Mindy," I said, "sounds like you've found a great job."

"Now, tell me about the wedding—I want to hear all the details."

"Wedding? What wedding?

Who's getting married?"

"Well, you and Mike, of course," I said.

"When's the big day?"

"*What* big day?" "Oh, come on Mindy," I said.

"How long have you two been together?"

"Eight years," she said, leaning back into her chair with a sigh.

* * *

"Eight years," I said, "and all that time you've been planning to get married as soon as you finished school.

Right?"

"Yeah," she said, "but things are different now."

"Different? How?"

"You must be joking—didn't you hear what I just said—about the job, the salary, the apartment, the Mercedes and the makeover?

Why would I want to get married, now that I've got all that?"

* * *

"I don't need a man anymore," she said. "I need a social secretary.

Hey, you wouldn't be interested in the job, would you?"

"Me—a social secretary?" I said.

"Are you serious?"

"Yes," she said, "I promise you—it'll be lots of fun."

"Maybe so," I said, "but I hate to think about my *own* social life—why would I want to arrange one for somebody else?"

"Are you sure?" Mindy said.
"I mean you *must* be nearly penniless after all that time in the *psycho* hospital.

Besides, I bet I'm the only person who would hire you now."

I felt the quicksand tugging at my feet, but I kicked it off.

* * *

"And don't forget," Mindy said, as she glanced doubtfully at my little two-bedroom farmhouse.

"You've got to keep this place up, and that'll take some serious money."

* * *

"I don't know," I said.

"I'm already taking two courses this semester, and I'm volunteering at the brain bio clinic, so I'm pretty busy.

But listen," I said, "if I hear of anyone looking for a job, I'll send them straight to you."

"Oh well," she said, "I guess it's up to you."

* * *

"So, how are things with you and Mike?" I asked, as I took a sip of tea.

"Well, to tell you the truth," she said, "we're not getting along very well."

"Oh, no—why?"

"I don't know exactly, but Mike can be difficult sometimes. Oh, don't get me wrong—I know he's a wonderful guy."

"That's right," I said, "I don't see how you could do any better."

"Believe me—I know," she said.

"Mike's been great for me. He's sweet and smart and considerate, and I know he's the best blacksmith in the whole area. He really wants to get ahead, but he's been working on his undergraduate degree for over six years now.

Besides, even if he works his tail off, he'll be lucky to see $25,000 this year."

"*I'm* making way more than that, and I'm just starting out."

"God bless him," I said.

"Listen—I'll help him buy a new truck and find a place to live, but that's *all* I can do—I just can't give anything else."

* * *

"Is that the whole story, Mindy?" I said, looking her in the eye.

"What do you mean?" "Well, I can't help but wonder—is there someone else in the picture?"

"Oh, no," she said, "at least not yet, but—mark my words—there will be somebody soon.

I'm not going to be alone for a long time. I'm going to find a man who is more. . .how should I say it. . .more . . . appropriate for me."

"More appropriate?

You mean someone with a better education, a higher social standing and, of course, more money. Is that what you mean?"

"Well. . .yes," she said.

* * *

I excused myself and went to the kitchen for a cup of coffee. It was strong and hot and wonderful, so I lingered for a few minutes before I went back outside.

* * *

I sat down across from her again.

"Mindy," I said, "have you told Mike how you feel?"

"Not really—I mean I've tried, but he just tells me to take some time to think it over.

So, I'm supposed to be thinking it over, but truth is, I've already made up my mind.

Mike and I will have to go our separate ways. I just have to wait until he gets used to the idea."

"He'll be devastated," I said.

"Oh, I know—it'll hurt terribly at first," she said, "but Mike bounces back quickly. It won't take him long to recover.

Besides, he never holds a grudge.

That'll make it much easier for me," she said, "I won't have to feel so guilty about leaving him behind."

* * *

We shifted the conversation to lighter things—the most beautiful butterflies in the garden, a great new restaurant in Princeton, and the local music festival.

* * *

We were quiet for a while, but Mindy broke the silence.

"Tell me about the *psycho* hospital," she said, leaning forward in her chair.

"You mean the *psych* hospital, don't you Mindy?"

"Oh, right," she said.

"Well, anyway—what was it like?"

I told her about the meds, the therapy, the other patients, and the ECT.

* * *

"Oh, my *God*," I said suddenly.

"What's the matter?"

"Nothing really," I said, "but talking about all that made me realize how sick I really was. I mean I knew I had problems, but I never thought I could get *that* bad."

* * *

Mindy flicked a mosquito from the cuff of her crisp, white linen shirt and glanced over at me.

"Well," she said, "I'm not surprised.

I figured you'd be dead by the time you were forty."

* * *

My mother used to tell me to forgive people who said things like that, but I just couldn't bring myself to do it.

* * *

Mindy waved good-bye as she pulled out of the driveway and went on her way.

'Well, there she goes,' I thought, 'a gigantic pile of narcissistic trash.'

`

www.ingramcontent.com/pod-product-compliance
Lightning Source LLC
Chambersburg PA
CBHW050856150626
46549CB00013B/2247